Sports Build Character

PERSEVERANCE IN SPORTS

by Todd Kortemeier

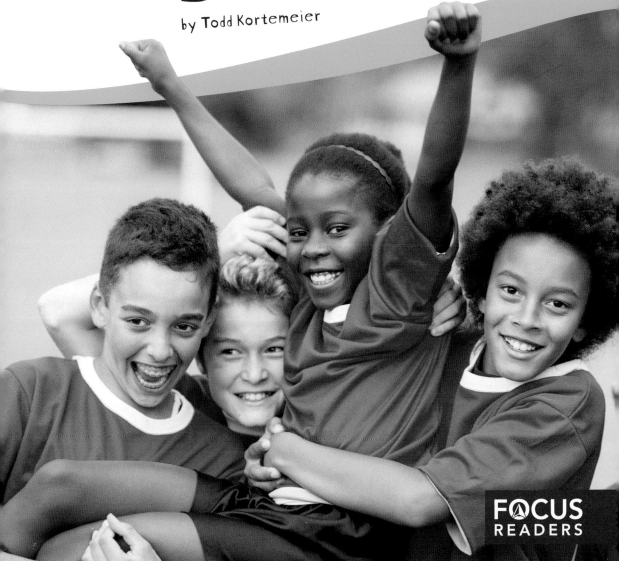

FOCUS READERS

www.focusreaders.com

Focus Readers is distributed by North Star Editions:
sales@northstareditions.com | 888-417-0195

Produced for Focus Readers by Red Line Editorial.

Photographs ©: FatCamera/iStockphoto, cover, 1, 25; SolStock/iStockphoto, 4–5; karelnoppe/iStockphoto, 7; Gene J. Puskar/AP Images, 8–9; Paul Sakuma/AP Images, 11; London News Pictures/Rex Features/AP Images, 12; Holger Bennewitz/Reuters/Newscom, 15; Ramon Espinosa/AP Images, 16; demarfa/iStockphoto, 19; Chris Williams/Icon Sportswire/AP Images, 20; Pixel_Pig/iStockphoto, 22–23, 29; gradyreese/iStockphoto, 26–27

ISBN
978-1-63517-533-2 (hardcover)
978-1-63517-605-6 (paperback)
978-1-63517-749-7 (ebook pdf)
978-1-63517-677-3 (hosted ebook)

Library of Congress Control Number: 2017948108

Printed in the United States of America
Mankato, MN
November, 2017

About the Author

Todd Kortemeier is a writer and editor from Minneapolis. He has written more than 50 books for young people, primarily on sports topics.

TABLE OF CONTENTS

CHAPTER 1

What Is Perseverance? 5

CHAPTER 2

Perseverance in Action 9

CHAPTER 3

Perseverance and You 23

CHARACTER QUESTIONS

Are You Persevering? 26

Focus on Perseverance • 28

Glossary • 30

To Learn More • 31

Index • 32

WHAT IS PERSEVERANCE?

Life is full of challenges. Some can be solved easily. Others demand a little extra effort. Athletes face challenges like these all the time. Some opponents are hard to beat.

It takes skill and confidence to take on obstacles.

The best athletes do what it takes to **overcome** any obstacle.

Athletes are used to pushing through hard times. That's what it means to persevere. Top athletes don't let anything stop them. Challenges may slow them down. But they keep going. When things are easy, athletes do not realize

LET'S DISCUSS

What are ways you persevere in a normal day? How do you do it?

> **Pushing through tiredness is one form of perseverance.**

their strength. They perform their best when things are toughest.

Perseverance takes courage and hard work. It means being ready for challenges. When hard times come, it means not giving up.

CHAPTER 2

PERSEVERANCE IN ACTION

Mario Lemieux scored a goal on his first shot in the National Hockey **League** (NHL). By 1993, he had been the league's top scorer three times. But that year, he was **diagnosed** with cancer.

 Mario Lemieux celebrates his 600th career goal.

 **Lemieux scores a goal in a 2002 game.**

Lemieux had dealt with injuries before. But this time, his illness threatened his career. He missed more than 20 games in the 1992–93 season. Even so, he led the league in scoring once again. He received the NHL's Masterton **Trophy** for perseverance.

But then Lemieux had more health problems. He needed back **surgery**. He also had side effects from cancer treatment. It was too much for Lemieux to handle. In 1997, he decided to retire.

But Lemieux made a comeback in 2000. He played for parts of five more seasons. He showed perseverance by never giving up.

> **Felicity Aston made her first trip to Antarctica at age 23.**

Felicity Aston was scared for two months straight. She was trying to cross Antarctica on skis. That was a distance of 1,084 miles (1,745 km). And she was doing it alone.

Aston was scared because so many bad things could happen. There were dangerously cold temperatures. Winds blew at hurricane speed. The ice had deep cracks she could fall into.

Aston was an experienced explorer. She had been all over the world. But this was her first **solo** trip. Being alone was her biggest challenge.

Each morning, she wanted to quit. She missed home. But she forced herself out of her tent and into the cold. She got into a routine. It made the miles pass easier.

Aston didn't feel completely alone. During summer, the sun never sets on Antarctica. So the sun was her one **companion**.

LET'S DISCUSS

Why do you think it was so scary for Felicity Aston to ski alone?

> Aston trained for Antarctica by skiing across Iceland.

After 59 days, Aston made it. On January 23, 2012, she became the first woman to cross Antarctica alone. Her perseverance paid off.

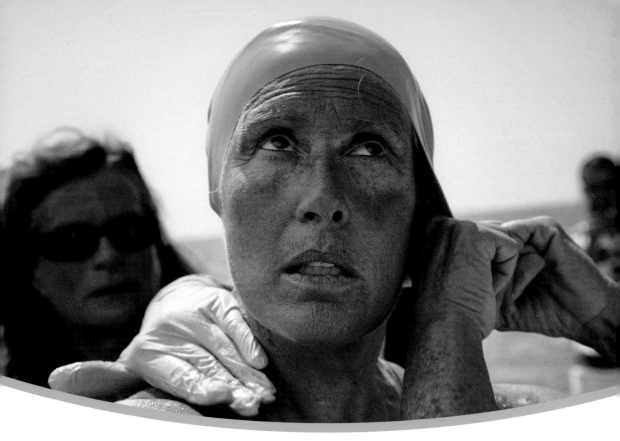

 Nyad adjusts her swim cap before setting out on her fourth attempt.

Swimming from Cuba to Florida involved a lot of risks. Diana Nyad knew that. But one thing kept her going. She always told herself to find a way.

Nyad had been trying to find a way since 1978. She attempted the swim four times. Each time, the elements beat her. Once, it was rough seas. Another time, it was a jellyfish sting.

Her first attempt came at age 29. Her fifth came in 2013, when she was 64 years old. She was not going to let age slow her down.

The swim was approximately 100 miles (161 km). It was a long trip. Sharks were her biggest fear.

Nobody had ever made the swim without a shark cage. Nyad had a team that followed her in a boat. But she was going to swim without a cage.

Nyad left Cuba on a Saturday morning. The wind was blowing, and the seas were rough. She told

LET'S DISCUSS

What would you have said to encourage Diana Nyad to keep swimming?

 Many swimmers and divers use shark cages to stay safe.

herself to keep putting one hand in front of the other.

Nyad got sick from too much saltwater. She was shivering from cold water overnight. But 53 hours later, she made it to Florida.

Romak's first major league game was in May 2014 against the Cincinnati Reds.

Any Major League Baseball (MLB) **debut** is special. It is a dream come true for the player. Jamie Romak had to wait longer than most. He was **drafted** in 2003. He didn't play an MLB game until 2014.

Injuries slowed Romak's progress through the **minor leagues**. Many stopped believing in him. But Romak never stopped believing in himself. In 2014, he finally got his chance with the Los Angeles Dodgers. Romak played in more than 1,000 minor league games before his first game in the majors.

LET'S DISCUSS

Can you think of an example of something worth waiting for?

CHAPTER 3

PERSEVERANCE AND YOU

Most things worth doing take perseverance. If you want to get an A on a test, you have to study. If you want to buy a video game, you have to save your money.

Cross-country running takes a lot of perseverance.

It's not always easy. That is when you need perseverance the most. Being able to persevere helps you push through tough times. You may not think you can do it. But if you try, you might surprise yourself. By taking many small steps, you can make it to the finish line.

LET'S DISCUSS

What is the hardest challenge you've had to face?

 You are often stronger than you think.

Life can be a challenge. Sports are a challenge, too. Not everybody can win. Perseverance doesn't always mean a win. But it does mean giving your all.

ARE YOU PERSEVERING?

Ask yourself these questions and decide.

- Do I practice tasks that are hard for me?
- Do I try again after making a mistake?
- Am I open to trying things in new ways?
- Do I ask for help when I need it?
- Do I encourage myself with kind words?

Next time you want to give up, challenge yourself not to. This might mean finishing a difficult book. Or it could be practicing a sport.

Focus helps you make it through hard tasks.

26

FOCUS ON
PERSEVERANCE

Write your answers on a separate piece of paper.

1. Write a sentence that describes how Jamie Romak persevered in Chapter 2.

2. Diana Nyad and Felicity Aston set records with their perseverance. What sport would you want to set a record in? How would you reach your goal?

3. In which year did Mario Lemieux make a comeback?
   - A. 2014
   - B. 1993
   - C. 2000

4. Why did Diana Nyad's crew follow her in a boat?
   - A. to make sure the water was warm enough
   - B. to keep Nyad healthy and safe
   - C. to give Nyad a place to sleep at night

5. What does **elements** mean in this book?

*Each time, the **elements** beat her. Once, it was rough seas. Another time, it was a jellyfish sting.*

    A. parts of a whole

    B. forces of nature

    C. painful injuries

6. What does **threatened** mean in this book?

*But this time, his illness **threatened** his career. He missed more than 20 games in the 1992–93 season.*

    A. helped

    B. was a danger to

    C. put an end to

Answer key on page 32.

GLOSSARY

companion
A person who keeps someone company.

debut
First appearance.

diagnosed
To have a disease recognized by a doctor.

drafted
Chosen by a team when entering a sports league.

league
A group of teams that play one another in competition.

minor leagues
The lower levels of a sport.

overcome
To deal with a problem successfully.

solo
Doing something alone.

surgery
A medical procedure to fix a problem inside the body.

trophy
A prize awarded for a certain achievement.

TO LEARN MORE

BOOKS

Antill, Sara. *Grit*. New York: PowerKids Press, 2014.

Herzog, Brad. *Powerful Stories of Perseverance in Sports*. Minneapolis: Free Spirit Publishing, 2014.

Shepherd, Jodie. *Perseverance: I Have Grit!* New York: Children's Press, 2016.

NOTE TO EDUCATORS

Visit **www.focusreaders.com** to find lesson plans, activities, links, and other resources related to this title.

INDEX

A

Antarctica, 12, 14, 15

Aston, Felicity, 12–15

C

Cuba, 16, 18

F

Florida, 16, 19

L

Lemieux, Mario, 9–11

Los Angeles Dodgers, 21

M

Major League Baseball,
20–21

Masterton Trophy, 11

minor leagues, 21

N

National Hockey League,
9, 11

Nyad, Diana, 16–19

R

Romak, Jamie, 20–21

Answer Key: **1.** Answers will vary; **2.** Answers will vary; **3.** C; **4.** B; **5.** B; **6.** B